TEENAGE MUTANT NINJA TURTLES®
ESCAPE FROM DIMENSION X

Illustrated by Isidre Mones

Adapted from a story by
David Weiss and Patty Howeth

Based on the Teenage Mutant Ninja Turtles
characters and comic books created by
Kevin Eastman and Peter Laird

RANDOM HOUSE
Happy House Group

Deep under New York City, Krang, the alien brain from Dimension X, held in his tentacles a blueprint for a robot body.

"Shredder, you idiot!" the brain said to his evil ninja partner. "You should be working on my new body, not wasting your time chasing some stupid *turtles*!"

The quivering brain continued. "My Stone Warriors are waiting in Dimension X to take over this planet. But I cannot let them see me like this!"

Shredder didn't care about Krang's feelings. "Dimension X...of course!" he thought. "A place of total war! I can get the weapons I need by pulling them through from Dimension X!"

The ninja ran from the room. "The Transdimensional Portal is complete!" he yelled. "Soon those blasted turtles will *die*! HA-HA-HA!"

"No! You fool!" cried Krang from his pedestal. "There's no telling what might come through!"

The Transdimensional Portal was a gateway between Earth and Dimension X. Shredder had used his workers and Krang's brains to build the device. But it hadn't been tested yet.

Shredder ignored Krang's warning. Standing at the portal control panel with his helpers Bebop and Rocksteady, he typed in the command OPEN PORTAL.

"YEEE-HAH!"

Two vehicles driven by aliens came flying out of the portal.

"What's this?" demanded Shredder. "Stop them!" he ordered Bebop and Rocksteady. But there was no stopping these cars. Using fiery laser beams, they blasted through the chamber wall.

"YA-HOO!" cried the aliens.

And then something else appeared in the portal...

...Krang's Stone Warriors!

"Boy! And I thought *we* were weird-lookin'," said Rocksteady.

BOOM! The giant stone men and their flying tank went crashing into the wall.

"You are Krang's Stone Warriors, are you not?" Shredder asked the fallen warriors.

"Yes," answered the angry soldiers. "So what?"

"So come with me!" ordered Shredder.

Meanwhile, the first two vehicles from Dimension X had burst out of the Technodrome.

Out for a drive in their van, the Teenage Mutant Ninja Turtles noticed something very strange. Two cars came flying out of a subway station!

"Jeepers creepers, man!" said Michaelangelo. "Like, what was *that*?"

"I don't know," said Leonardo. "But it can mean only one thing—the Shredder. Don, follow those cars!"

Back in the Technodrome, Shredder brought the Stone Warriors before Krang. The vain brain tried to cover himself with his tentacles.

"Lord Krang?!" exclaimed a warrior. "What happened to your body?"

"I lost it when I was banished to this miserable mudball," complained the brain. "What are you doing here, Traag?"

The Stone Warrior looked downward. "We were chasing the Neutrinos, Lord Krang, but they got away."

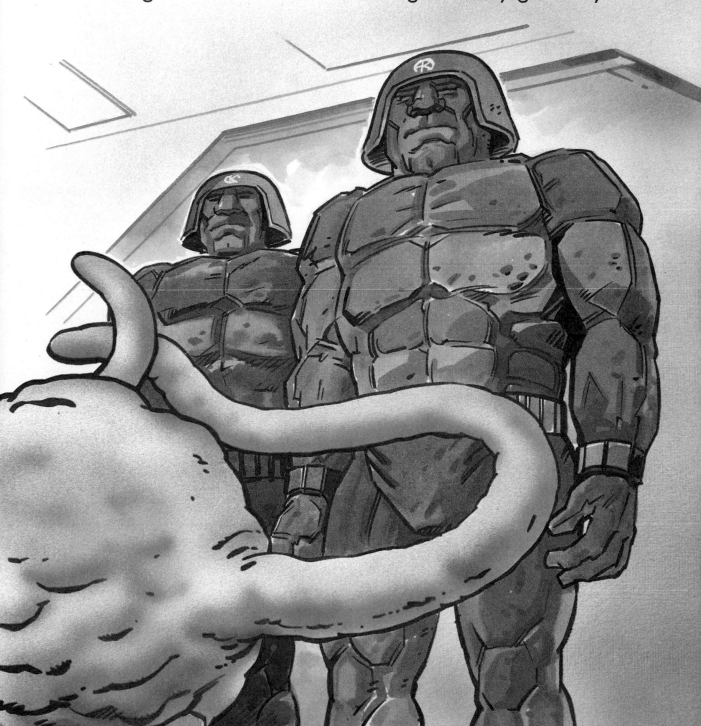

"Neutrinos…running loose *here*?" cried Krang. "Shredder, what have you done?"

"What do you mean?" asked Shredder. "Who are the Neutrinos?"

The alien brain's eyes flashed wildly. "They are juvenile delinquents from Dimension X! They hate war! They're a threat to all we stand for! And *worse*," the brain sputtered, *"they encourage people to have fun! They must be stopped!!"*

Meanwhile, on the street, the turtles were having trouble keeping up with the Neutrinos.

"Activate the turtle launcher!" shouted Donatello.

SWOOSH! The turtles flew through the air and landed in the vehicles.

"Okay buddy—pull over!" ordered Raphael.

"Let me go, daddy-o!" cried a Neutrino.

The Neutrinos landed their crafts.

"The Shredder must be getting pretty desperate to send kids like *you* after us," said Leonardo, checking out the young-looking Neutrinos.

"The who?" asked the aliens. "Dig, cats, one minute we're in Dimension X and then the next—POW!—we're in a room with some weirdo in a metal mask!"

"Hey, guys!" said Michaelangelo. "I think we're on the same side!"

The turtles took the Neutrinos into a closed game arcade. They needed to talk to the aliens without being seen.

"So what's your planet like?" asked Donatello.

"It's grimsville, man!" said a Neutrino, bent over a pinball machine. "All the grownups ever do is fight!"

"Yeah," added the Neutrino girl. "All we want to do is to have fun—but they never let us!"

KABOOM! Suddenly, a wall of the arcade came crashing down.

"All right, you Neutrinos!" yelled the Stone Warriors as their tank rode over the rubble. "Come on out!"

"Who are *those* dudes?" asked Raphael.

"Stone Warriors from Dimension X—they're very bad!" cried the Neutrinos.

The aliens headed for their flying cars, and the turtles jumped into the van. They sped away, leaving the Stone Warriors and their slow tank in the dust.

"We must get back and protect Lord Krang," one warrior said to the other. "Here, this Weather Maker will take care of those Neutrinos and the turtles with them!" The stone man hurled a Weather Maker—set for TOTAL CHAOS—into the sky.

When they were a safe distance away, the turtles and the Neutrinos stopped to make plans. But the turtle talk was cut short. It suddenly began to snow, *heavily.*
"Rock, dudes!" said Michaelangelo. "It's snowing!"
"In June?" asked Raphael.

"It must be a Stone Warrior Weather Maker!" cried one of the Neutrinos. "The snow will keep falling until it buries your city!"

"We'll have to deal with it later," said Leonardo. "We've got to get back to the Technodrome and stop Krang from bringing anything else through the dimensions!"

The Neutrinos and the turtles drove the flying vehicles to the Technodrome. They entered through the hole the Neutrinos had made earlier.

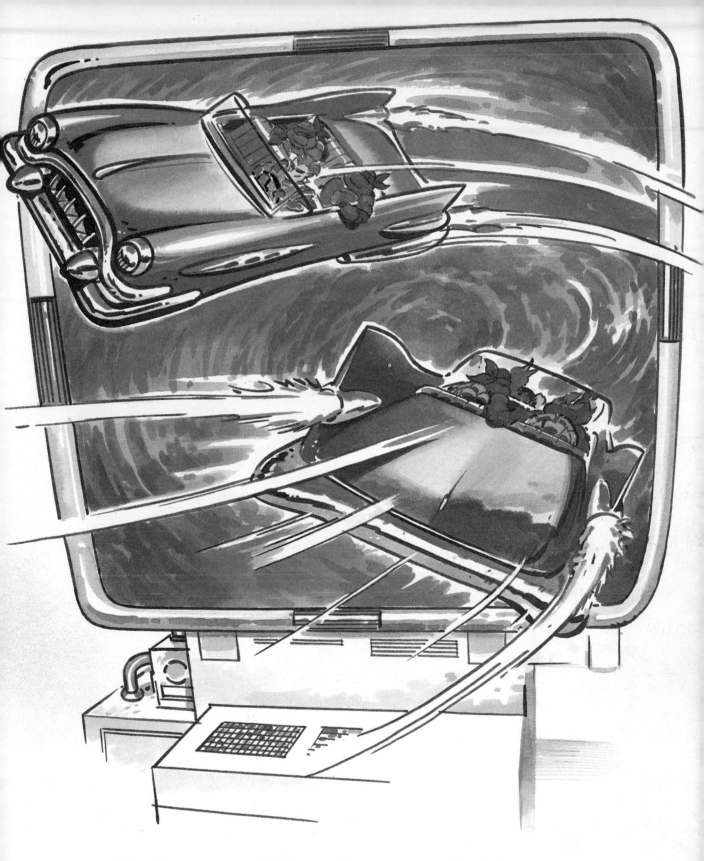

"Dig it, cats an' kittens," announced a Neutrino, swooping through the air in front of a huge screen. "The Transdimensional Portal!"

"You guys go find Krang," said Donatello. "Leo and I will work on opening the portal."

Traveling through the winding chambers of the Technodrome, Michaelangelo, Raphael, and their Neutrino driver began to pick up some strange life readings on the car monitor. Suddenly, the Neutrino made a sharp turn.

"Bingo!" he cried. "There he is...the brains of this operation!"

Krang sat on a giant glowing pedestal. Beside him stood his two Stone Warriors, their laser beam guns drawn.

"The monitor shows he's got a force field around him," said the Neutrino driver. "We'd better scram! Those guns will blow us to bits!"

"Catch you later, brain-breath!" taunted the turtles.

"After them!" Krang screamed to his warriors. He hysterically flailed his tentacles. "Don't let them get away!"

Donatello, meanwhile, was holding open the Transdimensional Portal.

"Hurry, you guys!" he yelled to the Neutrinos, who hovered together in a car nearby. "I can't hold it open too long!"

The Stone Warriors came running into the chamber. They headed straight for the turtles.

"Remember, team," said Leonardo. "Use their momentum!"

Just as the warriors were about to make contact, the turtles lifted them over their heads and— SWOOOSH!—tossed them into the portal. Instantly, they disappeared into Dimension X.

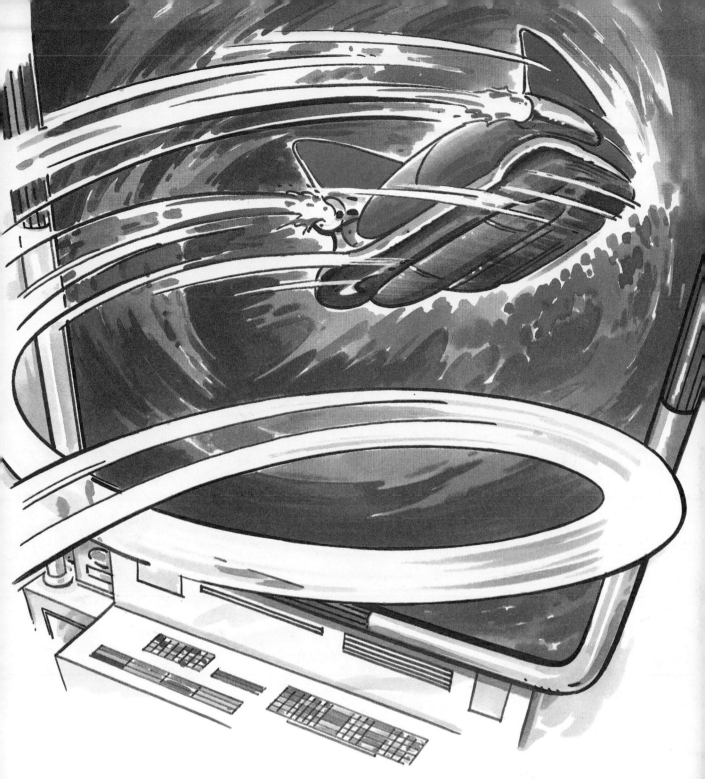

"Okay, Neutrinos, you're next!" said Donatello.

"It's been a blast, cool cats…" said the aliens. "We'd like to stay, but we've got to carry on the fight to have fun!"

The turtles quickly said good-bye. "We'll keep battling Krang here on Earth," they promised.

ZWISH! The Neutrinos were off. "So long, you crazy turtles!" they called.

"Come on, gang!" said Michaelangelo, jumping into the car left behind by the Neutrinos. "We've got no time to lose! That weather doohickey must be tearing up the city!"

The sun was shining over the city, but lightning flashed and heavy snow fell from the summer clouds.

"Pretty radical flying conditions, boys," said Raphael. "Hold on to your masks!" Donatello headed toward a funnel cloud that was forming in the distance.

Leonardo watched the snow piling up in the streets below. "This doesn't look good, guys," he said.

"I thought it might be in there," said Donatello as he flew the car up to the spinning funnel cloud. Lightning crackled from the Weather Maker, which was inside the dangerous cloud formation. "But how can we get to it without getting French-fried?"

"Like this!" shouted Leonardo. He jumped into the sky, his sword drawn.

"Leonardo, *wait*!" called Raphael. But it was too late. Leonardo fell through the sky, straight toward the Weather Maker. He easily sliced the machine to bits with his sword.

"HAI–YA!" he cried as he and the broken Weather Maker fell toward the earth. But instead of hitting the ground, he plopped into the backseat of the car.

"Nice catch, Don," said Raphael with a smile. "And nice work to you, too, Leo." The turtles laughed and began their descent.

But back at the Technodrome, there was no such merrymaking.

"All right, Krang," said the defeated Shredder. "I'll complete your body if that's what it takes..."

"Heh, heh, heh," chuckled the brain. "I'm glad you're seeing things my way."

But as Shredder turned his back to Krang, the evil ninja muttered to himself, "...if that's what it takes to destroy the turtles *once and for all*!"